Elizabeth's Enlightening Day at the Zoo

For Davon,

Betty R.

Betty R. Robinson

Illustrated by Floyd Yamyamin

Tellwell Talent
www.tellwell.ca

ISBN
978-0-2288-5757-0 (Hardcover)
978-0-2288-5756-3 (Paperback)

For Beth, who always brightens my day

Elizabeth: "Zahra, I'm so excited to be going to the zoo today! I love the zoo. I can't wait to see the wolves."

Zahra: "Me, too, and the reindeer."

Elizabeth: "I love the reindeer, too. Too bad we couldn't bring my dog. Rigel sometimes acts like she's a wolf.

"By the way, I love how your nail polish looks different when you move your hand in the sunlight. Is this one new? I haven't seen it before."

Zahra: "It is! It's one of my mom's new formulas. I love her choices of shades! She always gives me samples to wear. If you like this one, I'll see if I can get some for you."

Elizabeth: "Thanks! I'd love it.

"Oh good. We're almost next in line."

Zahra: "Why are barcodes always black and white? Why not different colours?"

Alex: "In a barcode, the black bars and the white bars make a pattern. So barcodes are all different, even though they kind of look the same.

"When you scan a barcode, the light from the scanner bounces, or **reflects**, off the barcode and goes back to the scanner. The barcode pattern has to be clear or else the scanner can't figure it out. Black and white give the best contrast, so we use black and white.

"Also, light reflects the most on white surfaces and the least on black surfaces made of the same material. Darker surfaces tend to **absorb**, or soak up, more light than they reflect. This also helps make the pattern clear."

Elizabeth: "Right, feel my black jeans, then your yellow jeans. Mine are much warmer from absorbing the Sun's heat than yours."

Zahra: "Do QR codes work the same way? They're black and white, too."

Alex: "Yes, they do."

Zahra: "Cool! Thanks!"

Elizabeth: "Your mom doesn't usually come with us on our zoo trips. Why today?"

Zahra: "She's designing a new line of nail polish, so she really wants to see the peacocks and the hummingbirds for inspiration.

"She also wants to see the special exhibit on flying squirrels, but I'm not sure what squirrels could have to do with colours for nail polish."

Elizabeth: "Mrs. Williams, you have such a cool job!"

Dalia: "I do! I love it! Using the science of colour and light to design my nail polish is so fun!

"Let's go to the Bird House first. I remember there's an information booth at the entrance. There might be information I can use."

Dalia: "Oh, that red is so brilliant."

Elizabeth: "What makes this feather so red?"

Danilo: "Good question! The colour of a bird's feather could be from a pigment right in the feather itself. Do you know what a pigment is?"

Zahra: "I do! A **pigment** is a type of material that's in my paints. Different pigments give me different paint colours."

Danilo: "Right! There are different types of pigment. The pigment in this feather gives the beautiful colour.

"The pigment absorbs all the colours in light except for the red. That's why we see the red–it doesn't get absorbed. And it gets reflected to our eyes, so that's what we see. Just like your blue T-shirt. All the colours in light except for the blue get absorbed, and the blue is reflected to our eyes."

Elizabeth: "My T-shirt is white. So all the colours are reflected because white light has all the colours, right?"

Danilo: "Yes, that's right."

Elizabeth: "You said the colour *could* be from a pigment. Is there another way?"

Danilo: "Yes, there is. Look at this peacock feather. See the different colours when I move it? This is called **iridescence**.

"Actually, like the way your friend's nail polish changes colour as she moves her hands in the light. The nail polish is iridescent.

"Feather iridescence happens with just certain types of feathers. So not all bird feathers are iridescent. Iridescent feathers have tiny layers of material inside. The light bends, or **refracts**, as it hits the layers. The refracted light gives different colours.

"And the light also gets reflected.

"So, like the nail polish, you see different colours when you move the feather."

Zahra: "Wow! I never knew I was iridescent!

"I see a peacock coming! Let's look at him."

Dalia: "Oh my! Isn't he beautiful? Look at that blue!"

Mom: "And the green!"

Elizabeth: "The peacock feathers are *so* iridescent. Look how they sparkle in the light!"

Dalia: "The amazing colours are an adaptation to attract a mate. You remember that an **adaptation** is a feature that helps an animal survive and reproduce? The male peacock shakes his feathers to make them sparkle more in the light. This attracts the female peacocks."

Zahra: "This is so cool. I think my science fair project this year will have something to do with light. Let's go inside the Bird House and see if there are any other iridescent birds."

Mom: "Look at that pink colour!"

Zahra: "And how iridescent those pink stomach feathers are! I can't believe this bright pink is on hummingbirds. I guess these wonderful colours are also to attract a mate, like the peacock.

"Mom, are you getting some ideas for your new line of nail polish?"

Dalia: "Yes. I have taken photos so I will remember all these beautiful colours. Next, let's go to the Butterfly House."

Zahra: "This blue is amazing! Wouldn't it be fun to have nail polish in this colour?"

Elizabeth: "For sure. These are blue morphos. They're from South America."

Zahra: "Is this blue colour another example of iridescence? Like with the peacock and hummingbird feathers?"

Elizabeth: "Yes, I've been learning about butterflies. Butterfly wings are different from feathers. But the way light acts is the same.

"The wings are mostly made of tiny scales. When the light hits the wings, the scales refract the light, and then reflect the gorgeous blue colour."

Zahra: "Oh, look! The other side of the wing isn't blue. It's brown."

Elizabeth: "The brown colour is an adaptation. The brown helps them blend in with their surroundings, and that helps them survive. So when the blue morphos are just sitting with their wings folded, a predator wouldn't see them as easily as when their wings are open.

"And the blue colour, another adaptation, helps them find a mate."

Zahra: "Amazing! Okay, let's go see the flying squirrels now. I'm curious to see what they have to do with light and colour for my mom's nail polish."

Dalia: "We're just in time! Did you see that squirrel's stomach?!"

Zahra: "It's such a bright pink. Is there a pink light shining on the flying squirrel?"

Elizabeth: "There *is* a light shining on the squirrel, but it's actually an **ultraviolet light**. Right, Mom?"

Mom: "Right. The squirrel's stomach is pink because the fur is fluorescing under the UV light.

"Have you learned about **fluorescence** yet, Zahra?"

Zahra: "Not yet."

Mom: "Something is fluorescent if light energy makes it give off light, or glow. Here, the energy from the UV light is making the fur on the squirrel's stomach give off pink light.

"Actually, since this squirrel is a living creature, glowing like that is called **biofluorescence**."

Zahra: "Okay. I can sort of see some squirrels. It is dark in here. But I can't see the pink unless the UV light is shining on their stomachs."

Mom: "That's right. Once you take away the light energy, there's no more glow.

"Let's head over to the Australia section. I heard in the news that the zoo has another surprise like the flying squirrels."

Zahra: "Look! A platypus! I saw a sign that says a platypus is a mammal, but it also lays eggs. It says people are mammals, but we don't lay eggs. So strange!

"And look, when it swims by the UV light its stomach glows green."

Elizabeth: "Just like the flying squirrel's stomach glowed pink. Biofluorescent. But there isn't much other information about why these animals glow."

Dalia: "When we're done here, let's head over to the aquarium. There's an unusual shark I want to see."

Chain Catshark, Atlantic Ocean (biofluorescent)

22

Dalia: "This is also new, like the flying squirrels. I heard about this. This is a chain catshark."

Elizabeth: "Some ocean animals, like jellyfish, make their own light. It's called **bioluminescence**. Is this shark making its own light?"

Dalia: "No, I don't think so. The sign here says the chain catshark is biofluorescent."

Zahra: "But there's just that light fixture at the top of the tank. The flying squirrels and the platypus had UV light shining on them."

Dalia: "These catsharks live on the ocean floor, so quite deep underwater. So deep that not much light reaches them. But some light does.

"The chain catshark absorbs the light that reaches it. Then it glows green. This is a fairly new discovery. Scientists think these sharks glow green so they can see each other better."

Zahra: "Elizabeth, I wish you could see yourself. Maybe I'll make you my science fair project."

Mom: "Okay, you two. Time to move on."

Dalia: "I have so many ideas now for my new line. Time to catch the Ah-Choo Zoo Train to see the reindeer and the wolves."

Elizabeth: "Bless you."

Zahra: "Funny, Elizabeth!"

ZOO CLINIC

2:30 pr
Gretta t
giraffe
Light
therap
foot

26

Elizabeth: "Hey, stop. What's going on here? What is the vet doing to the giraffe's foot?"

Mom: "This is part of the Zoo Clinic, or hospital. Gretta must have an injury on her foot.

"Oh, look. There's a schedule. It says she's getting light therapy."

Zahra: "Why the dark glasses?"

Mom: "Light therapy uses laser light. You don't want that to accidentally get in your eyes."

Zahra: "So lasers are dangerous?"

Mom: "They can be. **Lasers** are concentrated light, after all. The light used in this laser can go through the skin to help heal the injury, so it's important to protect your eyes. It can also make the injury hurt less. But this laser isn't hurting Gretta."

Elizabeth: "I'm glad we saw that! Let's catch that train now!"

Zahra: "I love riding the Ah-Choo Zoo Train."

Elizabeth: "Me, too. And here's the stop for the reindeer and wolves."

Zahra: "The wolves are so white. They must blend into the snow in the winter. I wonder if that makes it harder for reindeer to see them. I know wolves eat reindeer."

Elizabeth: "You know what? I did a science project about light, reindeer, and wolves. It actually isn't hard for the reindeer to see wolves in the winter."

30

Zahra: "Why isn't it hard for reindeer to see wolves in the winter?"

Elizabeth: "Almost everything, including trees and snow, *reflects* UV light. Especially the snow. So in the winter, when there's lots of snow, there's tons of UV light being reflected. But wolf fur *absorbs* UV light. Now, reindeer can see UV light. So the wolf looks dark to a reindeer. The dark wolf stands out against all the reflected UV light. The ability for reindeer to see UV light is an adaptation that helps protect them from wolves.

"And pee! All pee absorbs UV light. So to a reindeer, pee also looks dark against the snow. Hee hee! Another way for reindeer to spot a predator.

"*And* I learned that reindeer eat plants called lichen."

Zahra: "Let me guess: lichen also absorb UV light, so, to a reindeer, lichen also look dark against the snow? That helps reindeer find food in the snow?"

Elizabeth: "Exactly!

"Mom, have we run out of zoo time? Do we have time to go to the gift shop?"

Mom: "We have time. Next stop, gift shop."

Beep! Beep! Beep!

Mom: "Yikes! What's happening over there, by the penguins?"

Elizabeth: "Oh no! The penguins are escaping!"

Zahra: "Look, someone left the door to their pen open!"

Mom: "They think it's time for the penguin walk!"

Elizabeth: "Good thing they have that backup safety system set up!"

Zahra: "Where? What do you mean?"

Elizabeth: "Look–see the red light? When the penguins walk through the light, they break the light signal. That sets off the alarm we heard."

Dalia: "Looks like the zookeeper is getting them under control.

"We still have time for the gift shop!"

All proceeds go to the Zoo Clinic

34

Zahra: "Look at this glass hummingbird! It's like the one we saw in the Bird House.

"I have always been interested in learning how to make art pieces with glass. I love how light moves through glass. And how glass can be smooth like this, or it can have flat sections. You can control how the light acts."

Elizabeth: "And the colours, too. You can use what you know about light and colour, like your mom does with her nail polishes."

Zahra: "This visit to the zoo has given me ideas for my science fair project!"

Elizabeth: "When we get back to my place, do you want to brainstorm? I still have some books I used for my project, and some sites bookmarked on my computer."

Zahra: "That would be great! Thanks!"

Zahra: "Thanks for sharing your research with me.

"I really want to find out more about biofluorescence, especially with the flying squirrels. They're so cute! And my mom says this is a new discovery. I think I'm going to focus on that for my science fair project."

Elizabeth: "Great idea! You could make a really interesting project and maybe even use some of the photos that your mom took.

"But I know you're artistic. Will you make your own drawings?"

Zahra: "Maybe I'll do both."

Elizabeth: "I think I'll look into a light beam system for the backyard and Rigel. Mom says Rigel keeps going into the garden and she's not supposed to. Maybe I can set up a system like we saw at the zoo with the penguins that sends an alarm if she goes in the garden."

Mom: "We had a great time at the zoo today, Dalia."

Dalia: "We had a great time, too. What an interesting day! Those fabulous colours will definitely feature in my new nail polish line."

Elizabeth: "I'm so excited about your new nail polishes after today's trip, Mrs. Williams. Mom and I can't wait to see what formulas you come up with."

Zahra: "And I can't wait to help you name the different colours.

"Can we give some to Elizabeth and her mom when they're ready?"

Dalia: "Absolutely!"

Elizabeth: "Good luck with the science fair project, Zahra! Let me know if I can help."

Special Words in the Book

absorbs   soaks up, or takes in; wolf fur absorbs UV light

adaptation   a change in the structure or function of a living creature that helps it survive and reproduce

biofluorescence   the ability of a living creature to glow when exposed to certain light energy; flying squirrels are biofluorescent under UV light

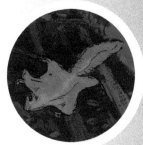

bioluminescence   the ability of a living creature to make its own light; some ocean creatures glow by making their own light

fluorescence   the ability of something to glow when exposed to certain light energy

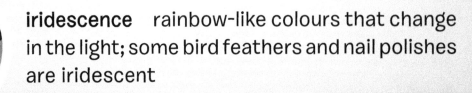

iridescence   rainbow-like colours that change in the light; some bird feathers and nail polishes are iridescent

laser light   concentrated light; light of one wavelength

pigment   a substance or material that gives an object its colour; paints and some bird feathers have pigments that provide a specific colour

reflects   bounces off of; light reflects off objects such as trees and snow and reaches our eyes so we can see them

refracts   bends, or changes direction; light refracts through glass and water

ultraviolet light   a type of light with higher energy than visible light; humans cannot normally detect UV light

CPSIA information can be obtained
at www.ICGtesting.com
Printed in the USA
BVHW020459090322
630959BV00003B/45